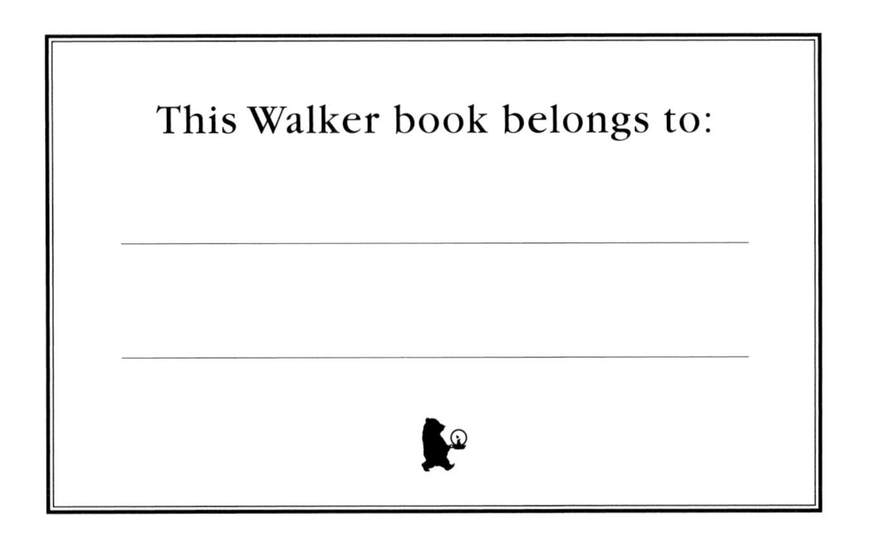
This Walker book belongs to:

SPAM

SPAM

To find out more about the Tower of London Ravens
please visit: www.hrp.org.uk

First published 2019 by Walker Books Ltd, 87 Vauxhall Walk, London SE11 5HJ
in association with Historic Royal Palaces, Hampton Court Palace, Surrey KT8 9AU

10 9 8 7 6 5 4 3 2 1

This book has been typeset in Garamond

Printed in China

British Library Cataloguing in Publication Data: a catalogue record for this book is available from the British Library

ISBN 978-1-4063-8529-8

www.walker.co.uk

AND THE RAVEN RESCUE

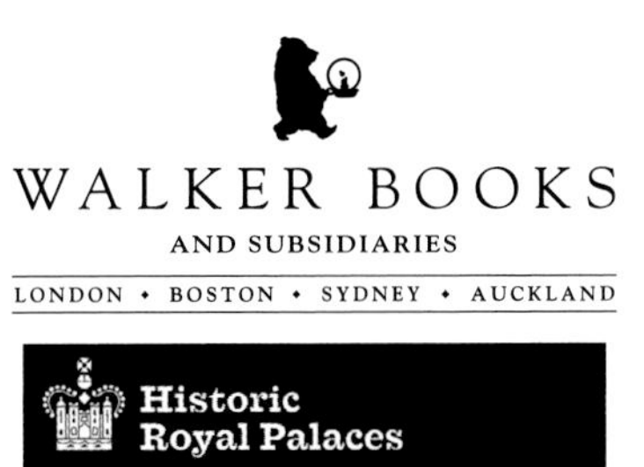

Rex gazed at the packet of crisps. He was starving.
And cheese and onion were his favourite.
But just as he started to nose towards the packet,
one of the Tower of London Ravens swooped down.
Rex wasn't sure about the bird's pointy beak and sharp
claws. Maybe he should try his favourite bin instead.

LITTER

It was almost the end of the day and the bin was overflowing with delicious, stinky rubbish. Rex jumped straight in. He could smell a sausage sandwich somewhere near the bottom.

He dug deeper and deeper…

Suddenly he was falling.
He went nose over tail, again and again,
until he hit the ground with a …

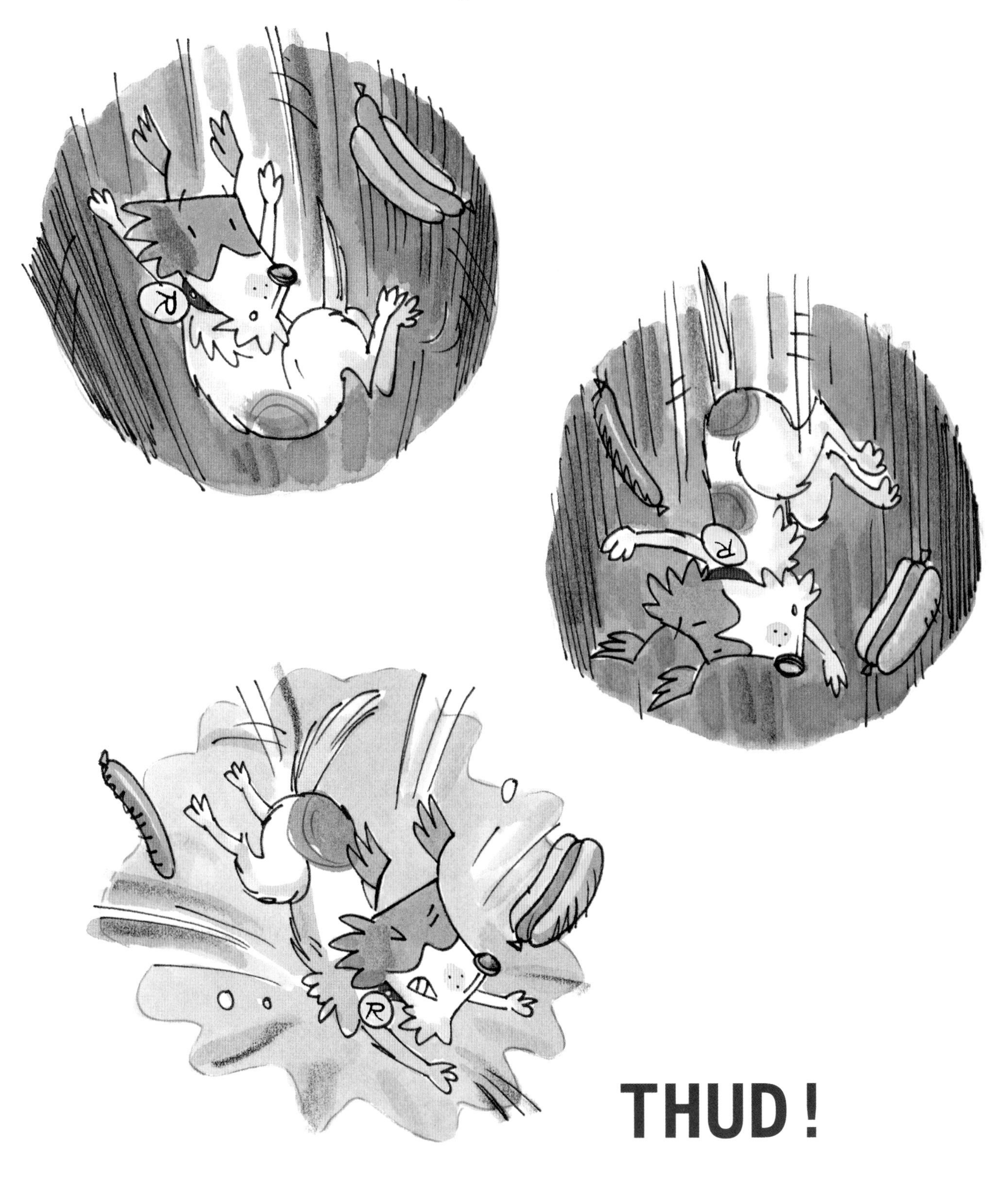

THUD!

Rex jumped to his feet in surprise. Everything looked different! The Tower's stone buildings were black with grime. The air smelled of burning and smoke was drifting off the river. A man wearing a strange tin hat was talking nearby to a Yeoman Warder. But before he could investigate, Rex got a whiff of the juiciest smell. He decided to follow his nose.

Just as Rex was about to wedge his nose into an empty tin, a dark shape dropped from the sky.

"You there! What do you think you're doing?"

"That's Crown Property. All thieves and spies will be imprisoned immediately!"

"I'm not a spy, I'm Rex! I live here. What's going on?"

"Hmmph. I suppose Rex doesn't sound like a spy's name," said the raven, looking slightly less cross.

“I’m Gripp, a Royal Raven in His Majesty’s Service! Don’t you know that Britain is at war? Night after night, bombs are dropped on the city. We only have the air raid sirens to warn us. The Yeoman Warders are trying to stop the Tower from being destroyed. ”

“But who gives you dinner?” asked Rex.

“The Tower’s closed to visitors, so there are no picnics, old boy. We’re very hungry.” said Gripp. “Come and see for yourself.”

"Meet Doris, Winston, Peggy, Ralph and Barbara," said Gripp.

"Keep calm and carrion!" cackled Doris.

"Things are quite desperate, old boy," said Gripp.

"We haven't had a proper meal in weeks, so I'm going on a top secret mission tonight. I've heard there's a royal residence where there are still delicious pickings."

"But I thought that if you left the Tower, the kingdom will fall," said Rex. "The legend says so!"

"I'm not worried," replied Gripp. "You can look after the others if there's a raid." And with that, he flew off into the dusk.

That night, Rex didn't get any sleep. He kept an ear pricked listening for the sirens that would mean an enemy bomb was about to drop or the rustle of feathers that would mean Gripp had returned.

As the sun came up, the ravens chattered anxiously among themselves. "Rex," said Winston eventually. "We know you're only a dog, but we need your help. Gripp hasn't come back! The kingdom will fall – and we might starve. Help us find him!"

"Leave it with me!" Rex wagged his tail.

Rex ran through London's streets.

"Have you seen a raven?" he barked.
"One flew in the direction of Buckingham Palace. Grumpy kind of chap! Go left at Piccadilly Circus," said a handsome whippet.
"But watch out!"

Rex scrabbled forward as a chunk of stone from a building fell to the street with a crash.
"It's your lucky day," said the whippet.
"Be careful now! And listen out for sirens."

Finally Rex reached an enormous pair of gates.
Gosh, this looks grand, he thought.
How did Gripp think he could sneak in here?

Rex darted past the guards as quickly as he could. Somewhere inside the palace, he could hear a dog barking. He raced towards the sound.

Rex found himself inside the palace kitchens.
A corgi had cornered Gripp and was yapping furiously.

"You trespassing crow! Wait till my mistress hears about this! Those buns belong to the Crown, not to thieving vermin like you!"

"Who are you calling vermin? You're not much bigger than a rat yourself, you cheeky pup! I'll give you trespass!" squawked Gripp, jabbing at the corgi with his beak.

Rex thought this was the moment to explain.
"That's not a crow. His name is Gripp
and he's a Royal Raven from the Tower of London."
The corgi quickly let go of Gripp's tail feathers.
"He's here to find food for his friends.
They're protecting the Tower and there isn't much
to eat," Rex said.
"Oh! Why didn't you say!" said the corgi.

A girl dashed into the kitchen. "Dookie, why are you making such a racket? Papa is trying to write a speech! What are you doing here?" said the girl to Gripp. "You're a Tower raven, aren't you?"

Gripp quickly fluffed up his feathers and stood to attention. "Mind your manners," he muttered to Rex. "That's Princess Elizabeth!"

"Have you come from the Tower looking for food?" Princess Elizabeth asked. "That's very daring. We can't have you going hungry when you are protecting the kingdom and serving my family. Let me give you some rations to take back. Quick before Cook sees!"

"You can carry it, can't you," the princess said, ruffling Rex's ears. "Have this as a token of my thanks." She took a gold charm off her bracelet and attached it to his collar. Rex barked his approval. It was time for him and Gripp to get back to the others.

Dusty and tired, Rex walked back to the Tower.
Gripp flew high above him.
They saw the others watching from the fortress.
“Gripp, we’re so glad you’re back,” said Peggy.
“Are they cucumber sandwiches?”
said Ralph in delight.

SPAM

"Thanks, Rex! You saved the day.
Will you stay for tea?" asked Barbara.
Rex's nose suddenly started twitching.
"That's very kind, but I need to go home.
Now, where's that bin?"

Rex jumped back inside.
He scrabbled all the way down to the bottom and suddenly he was falling.

He went nose over tail again and again, until he hit the ground with a …

THUD!

CHEESE ONION
LITTER

He looked around.
The Tower looked like it normally did.
Rex shook himself. His collar jingled.
How strange, Rex thought.
Then he saw the charm glinting in the sun.
"Dinner time!" he heard.
I hope there will be buns, he thought.

Also available from Walker Books:

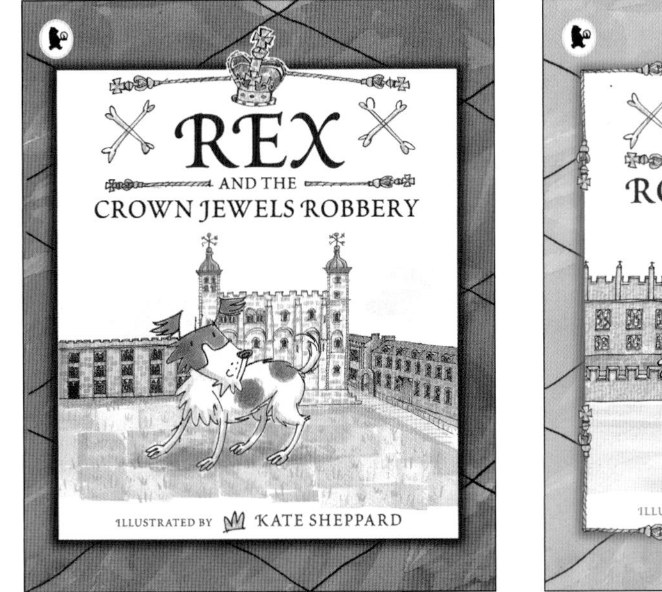

ISBN: 978-1-4063-6069-1

ISBN: 978-1-4063-6607-5

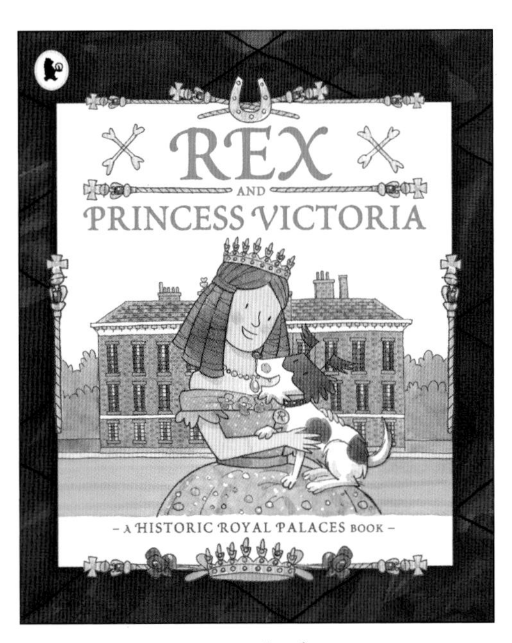

ISBN: 978-1-4063-7299-1